The Dragons of Peking

and other stories

Miles
Kelly

First published in 2011 by Miles Kelly Publishing Ltd
Harding's Barn, Bardfield End Green, Thaxted, Essex, CM6 3PX, UK

2 4 6 8 10 9 7 5 3 1

Publishing Director Belinda Gallagher
Creative Director Jo Cowan
Editor Amanda Askew
Senior Designer Joe Jones
Production Manager Elizabeth Collins
Reprographics Anthony Cambray, Stephan Davis, Lorraine King, Jennifer Hunt

ISBN 978-1-84810-498-3

Printed in China

British Library Cataloguing-in-Publication Data
A catalogue record for this book is available from the British Library

ACKNOWLEDGEMENTS
Artworks are from the Miles Kelly Artwork Bank

Cover artwork by Mike Phillips (Beehive Illustration)

Every effort has been made to acknowledge the source and copyright holder of each picture.
Miles Kelly Publishing apologises for any unintentional errors or omissions.

Made with paper from a sustainable forest
www.mileskelly.net
info@mileskelly.net

www.factsforprojects.com

Contents

The Dragons of Peking 4

Fairy Ointment 11

The Prince with the Nose 16

Persephone and the
    Pomegranate Seed 26

Rip Van Winkle 34

The Dragons of Peking

A Chinese folk tale

ONCE THERE WAS a poor prince who ruled over a group of peasants, living in a cluster of wooden huts in some dry, dusty fields. This sad little place was called Peking. However, the prince was good-hearted and determined, and had grand dreams of building Peking into a splendid city. The first thing he did was work hard with the men, women and children to build a high, solid wall with broad gates to keep enemies out.

The people were delighted. Little did they know that with all their digging, clearing, carrying and building, they'd disturbed two dragons who'd been asleep in an underground cave for thousands of years. You can imagine how grumpy the dragons felt when they were woken from their lovely long nap! "Who does this prince think he is," the first dragon growled, "getting his people to come banging around our cave like that!"

"Let's teach them all a lesson," the second dragon snorted.

That night, the two dragons wove a spell, turning themselves into an old man and an old woman. They stole away to the prince's house and, using magic, they crept past the royal guards, through several locked doors, into the very room where the prince lay, snoring soundly. The wrinkled couple asked, "O wise and gracious lord, we have come to ask your permission to leave your city of Peking and to take two baskets of water with us."

The prince stirred and murmured, "Why, of course you may," before falling back into a deep sleep.

The old man and woman hurried off to the river excitedly. It was narrow and muddy, but it was Peking's main source of water. They dipped their baskets into the stream and in minutes the river dwindled to a trickle, then dried up completely. Unbeknown to the prince, the disguised dragons' water baskets were enchanted – even if an entire ocean were poured into them, they would never be filled.

Next, the old man and woman took their water

baskets, which were no heavier than before, off to the village spring. Soon, instead of a bubbling gush of water, there was just a muddy puddle. Then they visited every house in the village, draining all the water baskets of every last drop. Finally, the stooped pair hobbled off with their water baskets down the road that led out of Peking.

By the time the sun rose, the wicked old couple were far away. Shouts of horror could be heard from all over Peking as the people woke and discovered that there was no water. Before long, there was a clamouring crowd outside the prince's house. "What shall we do?"

they shouted. "Our lips are parched. We can't boil any rice for breakfast. Our crops are withering in the sun before our very eyes!"

A stale smell wafted under the prince's nostrils. "Oh dear," he sighed, "has anyone been able to have a bath this morning?" The people shuffled about and looked down, red-faced.

Then the prince remembered his dream about the two old people and their water baskets. Being a wise person who believed in magic, he was very suspicious and dashed off to see his faithful old advisor straight away.

"Aha!" his advisor nodded with a knowing smile. Mumbling under his breath, he took the prince straight off to the dragons' cave outside the city. When the faithful old advisor saw the cave was empty, he said,

"Well, there you are then."

"Well, there I am then – what?" said the prince, rather frustrated.

"My father was told about this cave by his father, who was told by his father, who was told by–"

"Yes, yes!" cried the prince impatiently. "Please get on with it!"

"Two dragons were asleep here, who obviously weren't very impressed with your plans to improve the city. They've taken your water and gone!"

At once the prince called for his spear and his horse, and shot down the road in a cloud of dust. He thundered past many travellers until, after hours of hard riding, he recognized the old couple from his dream and reined in his panting horse. "I gave my permission for an old man and woman to take two baskets of water," the prince yelled, "not the two dragons that you really are!" He plunged his spear into each of their baskets and water immediately began to gush out in a cascading torrent.

With a spine-chilling roar, the old couple began to change back into dragons before the prince's horrified eyes. But before the fire-breathing creatures could pounce on him, they were swept off in one direction by the swirling waters, while the prince on his horse was carried off in the other. Everywhere was submerged under water, and the prince's horse scrambled onto a jutting crag that poked up out of the water. It had once been the peak of a gigantic mountain.

"Now what am I to do?" frowned the prince, dripping from head to foot.

"I shall pray to heaven for help," came a voice. The prince looked round in surprise and saw a Buddhist monk, who had been sitting there so silently that the prince hadn't even noticed him. The monk shut his eyes and bowed his head – and as he prayed, the waters vanished. The prince thanked the Buddhist monk earnestly and began galloping back to Peking.

As soon as the prince neared the city, the people came pouring out of the gates with happy faces. "You'll never believe it!" they cried. "All our water has come back. But best of all, a brand new fountain has sprung up. It has swelled the river with water more sweet and crystal clear than any we have ever seen!"

Thanks to the magical fountain, the land around Peking changed from being a dry, dusty wasteland to a beautiful, lusciously green paradise. The prince fulfilled his plans of making the city one of the most splendid in the world and, as far as the people know, the dragons have never come back.

Fairy Ointment

By Joseph Jacobs

DAME GOODY WAS a nurse that looked after sick people, and minded babies. One night she was woke up at midnight, and when she went downstairs, she saw a strange, little old fellow, who asked her to come to his wife who was too ill to mind her baby. Dame Goody didn't like the look of the old fellow, but business is business, so she popped on her things, and went down to him. And when she got down to him, he whisked her up on to a large coal-black horse with fiery eyes, that stood at the door, and soon they were going at a rare pace, Dame Goody holding on to the old fellow like grim death.

They rode and they rode, till at last they stopped before a cottage door. So they got down and went in and found the good woman in bed with the children playing about, and the babe, a fine bouncing boy, beside her.

Dame Goody took the babe, which was as fine a baby boy as you'd wish to see. The mother, when she handed the baby to Dame Goody to mind, gave her a box of ointment, and told her to stroke the baby's eyes with it as soon as it opened them.

After a while it began to open its eyes. Dame Goody saw that it had eyes just like its father. So she took the box of ointment and stroked its two eyelids with it. But she couldn't help wondering what it was for, as she had never seen such a thing done before. So she looked to see if the others were looking, and, when they were not noticing, she stroked her own right eyelid with the ointment.

No sooner had she done so, than everything seemed changed about her. The cottage became elegantly furnished. The mother in the bed was a beautiful lady, dressed up in white silk. The little baby was still more beautiful than before, and its clothes were made of a sort of silvery gauze.

Its little brothers and sisters around the bed were flat-nosed imps with pointed ears, who made faces at one another, and scratched their heads. In fact, they were up to all kinds of mischief, and Dame Goody knew that she had got into a house of fairies. But she said nothing to nobody, and as soon as the lady was well enough to mind the baby, she asked the old fellow to take her back home. So he came round to the door with the coal-black horse with eyes of fire, and off they went as fast as before till they came to Dame Goody's cottage, where the strange fellow lifted her down and left her, thanking her civilly enough, and paying her more than she had ever been paid before for such service.

Now next day happened to be market day, and as Dame Goody had been away from home, she wanted many things in the house, and trudged off to get them at the market. As she was buying the things she wanted, who should she see but the strange fellow who had taken her on the coal-black horse. And what do you think he was doing? Why he went about from stall to stall taking things from each – here some fruit, and there some eggs, and so on – and no one seemed to take any notice.

Now Dame Goody did not think it her business to interfere, but she thought she ought not to let so good a customer pass without speaking. So she went up to him, bobbed a curtsey and said:

"Good day, sir, I hope your good lady and the little one are as well as—"

But she couldn't finish what she was saying, for the

funny old fellow started back in surprise, and he said to her, "What! Do you see me today?"

"See you," said she, "why, of course I do, as plain as the sun in the skies, and what's more," said she, "I see you are busy, too, into the bargain."

"Ah, you see too much," said he, "now, pray, with which eye do you see all this?"

"With the right eye to be sure," said she, as proud as can be to find him out.

"The ointment! The ointment!" cried the old fairy thief. "Take that for meddling with what don't concern you – you shall see me no more." And with that he struck her on the right eye, and she couldn't see him anymore, and, what was worse, she was blind on the right side from that hour till the day of her death.

The Prince with the Nose

By Dinah Maria Mulock Craik

THERE WAS ONCE A KING who was passionately in love with a beautiful princess, but she could not be married because a magician had enchanted her. The king went to a good fairy to inquire what he should do. Said the fairy, after receiving him graciously:

"Sir, I will tell you a secret. The princess has a great cat whom she loves so well that she cares for nothing else; but she will be obliged to marry any person who is adroit enough to walk upon the cat's tail."

"That will not be very difficult," thought the king to himself, and departed, resolving to trample the cat's tail to pieces rather than not succeed in walking upon it. He went immediately to the palace of his fair mistress and the cat; the animal came in front of him, arching its back in anger as it was wont to do. The king lifted up his foot, thinking nothing would be so easy as to tread on the tail, but he found himself mistaken. Minon – that was the creature's name – twisted itself round so sharply that the king only hurt his own foot by stamping on the floor. For eight days did he pursue the cat everywhere: up and down the palace he was after it from morning till night, but with no better success; the tail seemed made of quicksilver, so very lively was it. At last the king had the good fortune to catch Minon sleeping, when – tramp, tramp – he trod on the tail with all his force.

Minon woke up, mewed horribly, and immediately changed from a cat into a large, fierce-looking man, who regarded the king with flashing eyes.

"You must marry the princess," cried he, "because you have broken the enchantment in which I held her, but I will be revenged on you. You shall have a son with a nose as long as this," – he made in the air a curve of half a foot – "yet he shall believe it is just like all other noses, and shall be always unfortunate till he has found out it is not. And if you ever tell anybody of this threat, you shall die on the spot."

The king, who was at first much terrified, soon began to laugh at this adventure. 'My son might have a worse misfortune than too long a nose,' thought he. 'At least it will hinder him neither in seeing nor hearing. I will go and find the princess, and marry her at once.'

He did so, but he only lived a few months after, and died before his little son was born, so that nobody knew anything about the secret of the nose.

The little prince was so much wished for that when he came into the world they agreed to call him Prince Wish. He had beautiful blue eyes, and a sweet little mouth, but his nose was so big that it covered half his face. The queen, his mother, was inconsolable. But, with time, she grew so used to the prince's nose that it did not seem to her any larger than ordinary noses of the court, where, in process of time, everybody with a long nose was very much admired, and the unfortunate people who had only snubs were taken little notice of.

Great care was observed in the education of the prince, and as soon as he could speak they told him all sorts of amusing tales, in which all the bad people had short noses, and all the good people had long ones. When he was old enough his tutor taught him history, and whenever any great king or lovely princess was referred to, the tutor always took care to mention that he or she had a long nose. All the royal apartments were filled with pictures and portraits having this peculiarity, so that at last Prince Wish began to regard the length of his nose as his greatest perfection.

When he was twenty years old his mother and his people wished him to marry. They procured for him the portraits of many princesses, but the one he preferred was Princess Darling, daughter of a powerful monarch and heiress to several kingdoms. Alas! With all her beauty, this princess had one great misfortune, a little turned-up nose. However, one clever person struck out a bright idea. He said that though it was necessary for a man to have a great nose, women were different, and that a learned man had discovered in a very old manuscript that the celebrated Cleopatra, queen of Egypt, the beauty of the ancient world, had a turned-up nose. At this information Prince Wish was so delighted that he immediately sent off ambassadors to demand Princess Darling in marriage.

She accepted his offer at once, and returned with the ambassadors. He made all haste to meet and welcome her, but when she was only three leagues distant from his capital, before he had time even to kiss her hand, the magician who had once assumed the shape of his mother's cat, Minon, appeared in the air and carried her off before the lover's very eyes.

Prince Wish, almost beside himself with grief, declared that nothing should induce him to return to his kingdom till he had found Princess Darling. He mounted a good horse, laid the reins on the animal's neck, and let him take him wherever he would.

The horse entered a wide, extended plain, and trotted on steadily the whole day without finding a single house. Master and beast began almost to faint

with hunger, and Prince Wish might have wished himself safe at home again, had he not discovered, just at dusk, a cavern, where sat a little woman who might have been more than a hundred years old.

She put on her spectacles the better to look at the stranger, and he noticed that her nose was so small that the spectacles would hardly stay on. Then the prince and the fairy – for it was a fairy – burst into a mutual fit of laughter.

"What a funny nose!" cried the one.

"Not so funny as yours, madam," returned the other. "But pray let us leave our noses alone, and be good enough to give me something to eat, for I am dying with hunger, and so is my poor horse."

"With all my heart," answered the fairy. "Although your nose is ridiculously long, you are no less the son of one of my best friends. I loved your father like a brother. He had a very handsome nose."

"What is wanting to my nose?" asked Wish.

"Oh! Nothing at all. On the contrary, there is a great deal too much of it, but never mind, one may be a very honest man, and yet have too big a nose.

"I will give you some supper directly, and while you eat it I will tell you my history in six words, for I hate much talking. A long tongue is as insupportable as a long nose; and I remember when I was young how much I used to be admired because I was not a talker, indeed, my mother, for poor as you see me now, I am the daughter of a great king, who always—"

'Hang the king your father!' Prince Wish was about to exclaim, but he stopped himself, and only observed that however the pleasure of her conversation might make him forget his hunger, it could not have the same effect upon his horse, who was really starving.

The fairy, pleased at his civility, called her servants and bade them supply him at once with all he needed. "And," added she, "I must say you are very polite and very good-tempered, in spite of your nose."

'What has the old woman to do with my nose?' thought the prince. 'If I were not so very hungry I would soon show her what she is – a regular old gossip and chatterbox. She fancies she talks little, indeed! One must be very foolish not to know one's own defects. This comes of being born a princess. Flatterers have spoiled her, and persuaded her that she talks little.'

While the prince thus meditated, the servants were laying the table, the fairy asking them a hundred questions, simply for the pleasure of hearing herself talk. 'Well,' thought Wish, 'I am delighted that I came hither, if only to learn how wise I have been in never listening to flatterers, who hide from us our faults, or make us believe they are perfections. But they could never deceive me. I know all my own weak points, I trust.' And truly he believed he did.

So he went on eating contentedly, nor stopped till the old fairy began to address him.

"Prince," said she, "will you be kind enough to turn a

little? Your nose casts such a shadow that I cannot see what is on my plate. And, as I was saying, your father admired me and always made me welcome at court. What is the court etiquette there now? Do the ladies still go to assemblies, promenades, balls? I beg your pardon for laughing, but how very long your nose is."

"I wish you would cease to speak of my nose," said the prince, becoming annoyed. "It is what it is, and I do not desire it any shorter."

"Oh! I see that I have vexed you," returned the fairy. "Nevertheless, I am one of your best friends, and so I shall take the liberty of always—"

She would doubtless have gone on talking till midnight, but the prince, unable to bear it any longer, here interrupted her, thanked her for her hospitality, bade her a hasty adieu, and rode away.

He travelled for a long time, half over the world, but he heard no news of Princess Darling. However, in each place he went to, he heard one remarkable fact – the great length of his own nose. The little boys in the streets jeered at him, the peasants stared at him, and the more polite ladies and gentlemen whom he met in society used to try in vain to keep from laughing, and to get out of his way as soon as they could. So the poor prince became gradually quite forlorn and solitary. He thought all the world was mad, but still he never thought of there being anything queer about his nose.

At last the old fairy, who, though she was a chatterbox, was very good-natured, saw that he was almost breaking his heart. She felt sorry for him, and wished to help, for she knew the enchantment, which hid from him the Princess Darling, could not be broken till he discovered his own defect. So she went in search of the princess, and being more powerful than the magician, she took her away from him, and shut her up in a palace of crystal, which she placed on the road which Prince Wish had to pass.

He was riding along, very melancholy, when he saw the palace, and at its entrance was a room made of

glass, in which sat his beloved princess, smiling and beautiful as ever. He leaped from his horse, and ran towards her. She held out her hand for him to kiss, but he could not get at it for the glass. Transported with eagerness and delight, he dashed his sword through the crystal, and succeeded in breaking a small opening, to which she put up her beautiful rosy mouth. But it was in vain, Prince Wish could not approach it. He twisted his neck about, and turned his head on all sides, till at length, putting up his hand to his face, he discovered the impediment.

"It must be confessed," exclaimed he, "that my nose is too long."

That moment the glass walls all split asunder, and the old fairy appeared, leading Princess Darling.

"Admit, prince," said she, "that you are very much obliged to me, for now the enchantment is ended. You may marry the object of your choice. But," added she, smiling, "I fear I might have talked to you forever on the subject of your nose, and you would not have believed me in its length, till it became an obstacle to your own inclinations. Now behold it!" and she held up a crystal mirror. Are you satisfied to be no different from other people?"

"Perfectly," said Prince Wish, who found his nose had shrunk to an ordinary length. And, taking the Princess Darling by the hand, he kissed her, courteously, affectionately, and satisfactorily. Then they departed to their own country, and lived very happy all their days.

Persephone and the Pomegranate Seed

An ancient Greek myth

OF ALL THE GODS and goddesses on Mount Olympus, Demeter loved the earth and its mortals the most. The great goddess of the harvest, she taught people how to plant, raise and reap grain, fruits and vegetables. In return, mortals loved Demeter dearly. Each mealtime, farmers' wives would set an extra place at the table, hoping that the goddess would grace them with her presence.

Demeter and the mighty father of the gods, Zeus, had a daughter, Persephone, who was their greatest joy. A beautiful girl, she cherished the earth, just like her mother. Persephone delighted in roaming the world, picking wild flowers in sunny meadows, and appreciating the splendour and beauty all around her.

One day, the goddess of love and beauty, Aphrodite, looked down from Mount Olympus. She smiled, catching sight of Persephone and her two best friends, the goddesses Athene and Artemis, enjoying themselves. Out of the corner of her eye, she also noticed the ruler of the underworld, Hades, riding through the sky in his black chariot.

Hades often left his dark kingdom to survey the earth above. The Titans, who had been imprisoned deep inside the world, were forever writhing about, trying to shake off their chains, and breathing fire in their fury. Hades had to watch that the earthquakes and volcanoes they caused were not tearing asunder the roof of his kingdom.

A sudden idea came to Aphrodite. She smiled mischeviously. None of the three goddesses, nor Hades, had ever been in love. But she could change all that. She quickly worked some magic, then sat back to watch the fun…

Sure enough, it wasn't long before Hades marched into Zeus' throne room. "Brother," the king of the underworld announced, "I am in torment. I have fallen deeply in love with your daughter, Persephone, and cannot rest for longing. I have come to ask for her hand in marriage. I swear that I will love her for eternity and do everything in my power to make her happy."

Zeus was pleased. The mighty king of a vast kingdom, Hades was a wise and fair ruler. He owned all the wealth of the earth, including diamonds and emeralds.

"I can think of no one better as a husband for Persephone," Zeus assured his brother. "However, I fear that Demeter will not allow it. She will never see her daughter taken from the sunshine that she loves to live underground – no matter how excellent a husband you are."

Hades groaned. "Brother, believe me, I know this too well – and I have tried my hardest to forget Persephone. My thoughts are filled with her, day and night. I can admire no other. If I cannot have Persephone as my wife, I fear my heart will break and I will never recover from such sorrow."

Zeus thought for a moment. "If asking Demeter will bring certain rejection, do not ask her. Seize Persephone and sweep her away. By the time Demeter finds out, it will be too late for her to do anything." Hades embraced his brother, then strode away, determinedly.

The very next day, Persephone, Athene and Artemis were laughing and playing in the woods, when in a clearing, Persephone spotted a flower she had never seen before. Delighted at its shimmering colours and delicate petals, she stooped to breathe in its sweet fragrance.

Suddenly, a thunderous rumble shook the earth and the ground opened wide. Out of underworld came a gleaming, black chariot pulled by two wild-eyed horses. Persephone tried to run but she was quickly seized by a strong arm and swept up into the arms of the dark lord himself. Hades had come to collect his love. Galloping faster than the wind, the horses sprang away across the earth.

Athene and Artemis fell to their knees in the quake, and didn't see Hades take Persephone. On hearing her scream, they span round to find that she had vanished.

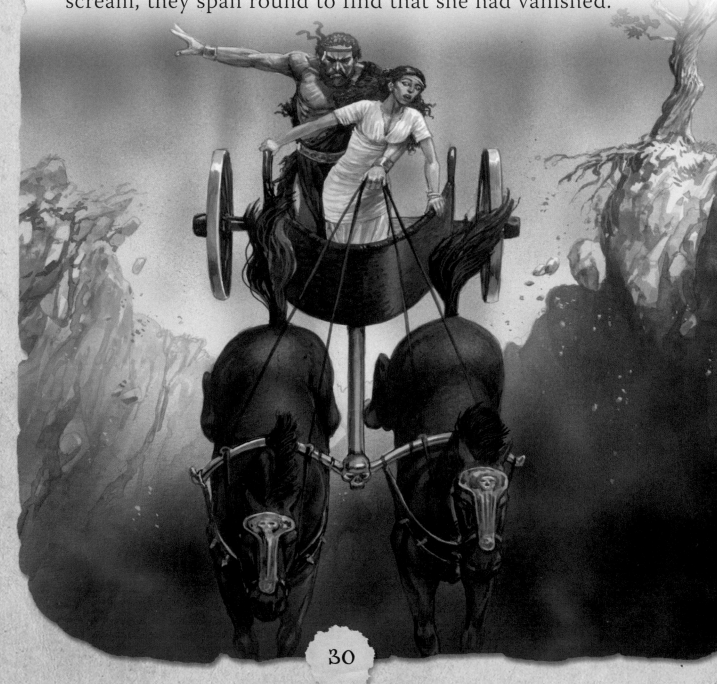

The bunch of flowers she had been picking were strewn around a gaping fissure in the earth. The panicked goddesses ran back and forth, desperately calling her name – but the only reply was the agitated bowing of the plants in the breeze and the alarmed rustling of the leaves.

Meanwhile, Persephone was held tightly in Hades' grasp as the chariot sped across fields valleys. Beside herself with terror, Persephone cried out, "Mother! Father! Help me! Someone, please help me!" But the lord of the dead simply cracked his whip, and they galloped through the sky, far away from the gods and goddesses of Mount Olympus. Persephone's voice simply faded and died on the wind.

Fortunately, the lord of the sun Helios was journeying in his own chariot high in the sky. For one brief moment, Helios saw the frothing horses, the grim-faced lord of darkness, and the horrified, screaming girl. Suddenly, the ground split in two, the horses and the chariot plunged down into the depths, and the earth sealed over them. Persephone was gone.

When Athene and Artemis told Demeter that Persephone had disappeared, the great goddess was beside herself with grief. Demeter set off across the whole world, desperately looking everywhere for her beloved child – but no one could tell her anything.

Demeter's sorrow soon turned to rage, and her anger turned on the earth and all the mortals it fed. The goddess commanded every seed to shrivel, every plant to droop, and every tree to wither. She ordered cold winds to blow, drying the soil. Then she told heavy rains to fall, washing away the earth's goodness. She prevented animals from giving birth to young. She ordered bushes not to bear fruit and vegetables not to sprout. She commanded leaves to fall from trees.

Helios saw what was happening from his chariot, high in the heavens. Deeply concerned, he hurried to Demeter at once to explain what he had seen. Demeter was not reassured or relieved at the news, and took out her fury on the entire world. Boiling with rage, she was determined to make all mortals suffer as she was suffering. She would leave them to die of starvation. Then the gods would be sorry.

Zeus was indeed alarmed as he beheld his dying world. He had underestimated Demeter's grief and wrath and immediately sent his messenger, Hermes, to the underworld. "Find Persephone and bring her back to her mother," Zeus ordered Hermes. "But hurry, for if she has eaten any of the food of the dead, she must remain in the underworld forever!"

Hermes sped into the kingdom of darkness. Kneeling before the thrones of Hades and his new queen, he explained that Demeter would destroy all creation if Persephone were not returned to the light at once. The sorrowful girl's heart was filled with hope at the messenger's words – until Hermes looked sternly at her and said, "Tell me, Persephone, that you have not yet eaten the food of the dead."

Persephone's heart began to flutter. "I have," she gasped, "but only one pomegranate seed – that's all."

The king of the underworld took Persephone's hand. "You now belong to me and my kingdom, but I will not force you to stay here forever," he said gently. "You must keep me company here for only half of every year. Now, go to your mother. But remember I love you."

Soon Persephone and Demeter were joyfully reunited. Touched by Hades' kindness, Persephone found herself thinking fondly of the sad king sitting alone in the underworld without her. She would be glad to return to him when the time came.

Every spring and summer, Demeter rejoices that Persephone is with her and the earth flourishes. But every autumn and winter, Demeter mourns her daughter's descent into the underworld, and the earth becomes barren once more.

Rip Van Winkle

An American legend

IN A VILLAGE in the foothills of the Catskill Mountains of America lived a man called Rip Van Winkle. Everybody liked Rip. He was a generous, easy-going man who was always glad to lend a hand to his neighbours. In fact, Rip Van Winkle was always to be found doing anybody else's work except his own. And didn't his wife remind him about it all the time! Nag, nag, nag it was, all day long. "Rip, if you're not too busy varnishing Mrs Green's fence today, you can mend the holes in the shed. Instead of helping to burn the farmer's rubbish, you can feed the chickens and milk the cows. Then if you can stop yourself from building Arne Jacob's wall for him, there's our potatoes to dig up and the wagon to be washed down and the gutters to be cleared out and the yard to be swept and…" And so it was every day, on and on and on and on.

Every now and again, Rip Van Winkle whistled for his faithful dog Wolf, shouldered his gun, and strode away from his wife without a word. Off he would stroll up the mountainside, along the river and through the pine forests until his wife's screeching voice had grown so faint that he could no longer hear it, and he was surrounded only by the twittering of the birds, the rustling of the trees in the breeze and the panting of his companion by his side. Rip always knew there would be heck to pay when he got home. But a day off in the peaceful sunshine was well worth it!

One day when Rip had disappeared on one of these rambles, he was taking a rest under a shady tree, when he heard a voice calling his name. "Rip Van Winkle! Rip Van Winkle! Rip Van Winkle!" came the high, shrill cry.

Wolf's ears flattened against his skull and he gave a long, low growl. Rip looked in the direction Wolf was snarling and there among the long grass was a nodding green feather. The nodding green feather was tucked into a bright red cap. The cap was on the head of a bearded man no higher than his own boot, struggling under the weight of a big beer barrel.

"Rip Van Winkle! Rip Van Winkle! Rip Van Winkle!" shouted the dwarf, crossly.

"Will you get yourself over here and give me a hand with this barrel before it squashes me!"

Rip was so used to doing what he was told that he jumped up to help at once.

"That's better," wheezed the dwarf, as Rip took one end of the heavy barrel. "Now up we go!" Rip nearly tripped over as the dwarf stomped away up the mountain, pulling the barrel and Rip Van Winkle with him.

After at least an hour's tramping and much huffing and puffing, the dwarf led Rip Van Winkle straight behind a thundering waterfall, through a hidden door and into an enormous cavern.

Dwarfs were swarming everywhere. Some were dressed in aprons, pouring endless tankards of beer out of big kegs just like the one Rip was helping to carry. Others were playing nine pins, rolling smooth round black rocks at copper skittles and cheering loudly. Yet more dwarfs were drinking and clinking their tankards together, singing noisy songs.

"Pull up a chair," Rip's new friend invited him, lowering the barrel to the floor and passing him a tankard. "Help yourself to a drink. You must be gasping thirsty after that climb – I know I am!"

The stunned Rip Van Winkle did just that. "My,

that's mighty powerful stuff!" he spluttered, as he swallowed down a huge gulp of the dwarf beer. "But whatever it is, it's very good!" He licked his lips and poured himself another tankardful. None of the dwarfs was taking a blind bit of notice of him, so Rip Van Winkle sat back and began to watch the nine pins competition. "Well, this is a most pleasant way to spend the afternoon," he thought, helping himself to another beer... and another... and another... and another. And before Rip Van Winkle even realized he was drunk, he had slumped forwards onto a huge flat rock and was snoring loudly.

When Rip woke up, the dwarfs were gone and the cavern was empty. "Come on, Wolf," he yawned, and they both stood up and stretched. "We'd better hurry back or we'll never hear the last of it." Through the little door they strode and out from behind the waterfall and off down the mountain. "Wait for it," he murmured to his dog as he climbed the porch steps to his house. "Any minute now, that wife of mine will start screeching fit to wake the dead." Rip put his hand on the doorknob and turned. He nearly walked smack-bang into the door as it failed to open. "Well, this needs a bit of oil," he murmured to himself. He rattled the knob and twisted it about. "Funny," Rip remarked, "I think it's locked. She never locks the door, never."

At that very moment, the front door opened and there stood a woman with an angry face. "Who are you?" the woman snapped. "What are you up to, trying to get in my front door?" She was not his wife. In fact, Rip Van Winkle had never seen her before.

"Who are you?" gasped Rip. "What are you doing in my house?"

"Your house!" the woman scoffed. "I've lived here for over nineteen years!"

Rip Van Winkle backed off the porch and looked around him. He scratched his head and stared. The woman was right – it wasn't his house. Well, it looked similar to his house, but the curtains at the window were different. There were strange chairs on the verandah. The wagon in the yard was not his wagon.

"But – I – How –" stuttered Rip. "Where's Mrs Van Winkle?"

"Mrs Van Winkle?" the puzzled woman gawped.

"She left here nearly twenty years ago, just after her husband wandered off and disappeared. Now, be off with you or I'll call the police!"

"Twenty years!" marvelled Rip Van Winkle, as he wandered away stroking his beard. His beard! Suddenly Rip realized that his beard hung down to his knees. The woman's words had to be true! He had been asleep for twenty years!

Rip Van Winkle's hands trembled with the shock as he reached down and patted the bemused Wolf comfortingly. Then his mouth began to curve upwards in a small smile. "Just imagine, Wolf," he murmured. "No more nagging – ever!" Rip Van Winkle turned and strode across the street, whistling a merry tune. Happily, the inn was in the same place it always had been – and when the townspeople heard his story, he never had to buy himself another pint of beer again.